Let's Go to

Caryl Hart

Bee and Billy,

Billy and Bee,

See what they

can do!

WALKER BOOKS
AND SUBSIDIARIES
LONDON · BOSTON · SYDNEY · AUCKLAND

For Mandy~C.H. ♥▲♥ For Julie T~L.T. ◆ First published 2017 by Walker Books Ltd, 87 Vauxhall Walk, London SE11 5HJ ◆ This edition published 2018 ◆ Text © 2017 Caryl Hart ◆ Illustrations © 2017 Lauren Tobia ◆ The right of Caryl Hart and Lauren Tobia to be identified as author and illustrator respectively of this work has been asserted by them in accordance with the Copyright, Designs and Patents Act 1988 ◆ This book has been typeset in Futura

Nursery!
Lauren Tobia

They're so
tumbly,
wiggly,
jumbly!

Can YOU
do it, too?

Climb the steps, **DING DONG!**

The blue door opens wide.

Look! It's Bee and Billy,

About to go inside...

Children shout
and giggle,
Mummies hug goodbye.

Bee dashes off
    to play postmen,
Billy is hidey shy.

"Billy, look,"

says Postman Bee.

"This letter is

for you.

It says, 'Dear Billy,

Come to the farm,

There's lots of work

to do.'"

They drive the train together,

Clickety-clickety-CLACK!

The sheep say,

"Baa!"

The cows say,

"Moo!"

What do the

ducks say?

"QUACK!"

Someone's got the tractor,

It's little Baby Boo!

Bee shouts,

"MINE!"

Then Baby cries,

Baby wants it,

too.

Clever big boy Billy,

Gives Baby Boo

his train.

Baby's giggly,

smiley, dribbly,

Happy once again.

Now, what's that sniff-a-licious smell?

It's something really yummy...

"Toast time!

Toast time!"

Bee shouts out.

She has a rumbly tummy!

Billy is munchy-crumbly-crunchy,

Grabs his spotty cup.

Buttery fingers slip and slide,

Milky cup tips up!

Poor Billy! He starts to wail,

Grown-ups mop and fuss.

Bee says kindly, **"Share my drink.**

There's enough for both of us."

Then Bee and Billy build a tower,

Wibbly-wobbly tall.

Red and green and yellow blocks,

Can you count them all?

Little Baby Boo crawls past,
Blocks crash to the floor.
"All fall down!" claps Billy,
And they build it up
once more.

Billy finds a shaker.

"**Oh yes!**" shouts Bee.

"**Let's sing!**"

Bee and Billy jump
and dance,

Then everyone joins in!

Mummy's back! Let's tidy up,

There are coats and shoes to find.

And where have Billy's
    socks gone?

We can't leave those behind!

Bee cries and shouts
    and stamps her feet,

She wants to stay
    and play.

But Mummy says,

"It's time to go,
You'll come back
another day."

Bee and Billy
are going home,
Today has been
such fun.

They're yawny,
sleepy, snuggly,
tired...

Goodbye,
everyone!

Also illustrated by Lauren Tobia:

978-1-4063-3841-6

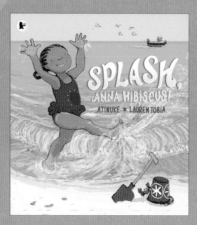

978-1-4063-5468-3

978-1-4063-7807-8

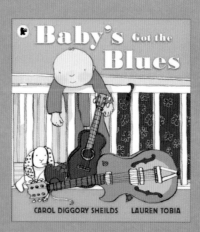

978-1-4063-6004-2

Caryl Hart is the author of more than thirty books for children.
She lives on top of a windy hill in the Peak District with her husband and two daughters.
Find her online at **carylhart.com** and on Twitter as **@carylhart1**.

Lauren Tobia lives in Bristol with her husband and their two Jack Russell terriers, Poppy and Tilly.
Find her online at **laurentobia.com** and on Twitter as **@laurentobia**.

Available from all good booksellers

www.walker.co.uk